The Rancher's Sweetheart

Cheryl Wright

Contents

Copyright © 2018 by Cheryl Wright

From the Author

He's been gone more than 18 years now, but I'll never forget the rodeos my dad (and mother) took us to as kids. We looked forward to going each and every year.

Born in the country (as we kids were), my dad was a country man through and through. His first ever job was at a rodeo. He went on to become a ranger, and a horse breaker, amongst other things. His brother looked after horses all his working life, including taking tourists on trail rides. Every now and then I managed to insinuate myself into those trips.

I grew up with horses, and the country ways of doing things. And I'm so glad I did.

Sadly, we moved to the city down the track, but I loved (and still love) horses so much, I spent nearly all my extra money and most of my weekends going on horse rides.

Thanks

Thanks to my very dear friends (and authors),
Margaret Tanner and Susan Horsnell.

Without their encouragement, this book would not
be written.

Thanks also to Alan, my husband of 43 years, who
has been a relentless supporter of my

writing for as long as I can remember.

Disclaimer

This book is a work of fiction.

Any resemblance to persons, living or dead, or
places, events or locales is purely coincidental.

The characters and towns contained within are
productions of the author's imagination and are
used fictitiously.

Although facts are found throughout, the author has
embellished or changed some for the sake of the
story.

Chapter One

Kody Callahan opened his eyes and gingerly looked around.

The last thing he remembered was riding his horse Cracker across the back paddock. He'd left home not long after sunrise, as soon as he'd finished his steaming mug of coffee.

Best time of the day for him. Not the coffee so much as watching the sun rise as he sat on a comfortable chair out on his front porch.

What a way to start the day! He turned his head and smiled, and the small movement caused him pain.

He tried to get up off the cold, damp ground, but a wave of dizziness hit him before he'd gotten very far, so he lay back down again. He covered his eyes against the sun momentarily. Sleep, that's what he needed sleep.

Yep.

Yeah.

Just. A. Short. Snooze.

When he woke again, he felt disoriented. Kody glanced around and saw his cowboy hat just out of reach. He tried to get to it. The excruciating pain in his head had him laying back down, but not before he'd retrieved his hat. He'd had that hat for as long as he could remember. He wasn't going to lose it now.

He ran his hand through his unruly brown hair to push it off his face and felt the huge lump on the back of his head. A wet and sticky lump. He didn't need to look at his fingers to know what it was.

"Cracker." He whistled, and the horse came to him, nickering into Kody's neck. "Yeah, boy. I know. Not a good situation." He half sat, as much as he could without passing out, and reached into his oilskin duster for his satellite phone.

Except it wasn't there.

"Damn it, Kody. You need to let someone know you're going out alone," his brother Sheriff Chase Callahan told him. "What if you hadn't made it back? It could have been days before anyone knew you were missing."

"You're just being stupid now," Kody told him, ready to storm out, except he wasn't in any condition to go anywhere. That knock on the head was apparently pretty bad. Bad enough for stitches.

"Don't get me started on stupid...." Chase looked at him knowingly. Kody knew he was right,

7

but if he told someone every time he went out alone, he'd spend all his time notifying folks of his whereabouts and would never get anything done.

Nope, wasn't going to happen.

"If you weren't such a damned loner, none of this would happen." Chase ran his fingers across the stubble on his chin. He hadn't had time to shave – he'd been dragged out of bed with the call from the hospital that Kody was in trouble.

Not that he'd minded, Kody was sure. They were brothers after all. More than brothers. Best mates.

He lay on a bed in the hospital emergency room, waiting for his head to be stitched. His feet dangling over the end of the bed.

In a flimsy white gown.

He groaned. It couldn't get any worse. Could it?

His other brother Rory entered the room. "What the hell, Kody?"

His concerned look touched Kody. The words that followed just annoyed him. "Geez man, get yourself a girl. At least she'd know if you didn't come home when you should."

Kody tried to sit up and protest, but his head screamed at him and the room spun. Rory took a few quick strides toward him and steadied him, laying him back on the bed. "Steady down. You probably have concussion."

"That's exactly what he has." The sweet feminine voice sang the words in Kody's disoriented mind, and he turned his face toward her. It hurt like hell. "Stay down please, Mr Callahan," she said as she moved toward him and felt around his head, checking for any other damage.

"We're admitting him for at least tonight, depending on how he is tomorrow." She spoke to Chase and Rory. "We'll do scans to ensure there are no other injuries. Falling off a horse can be incredibly dangerous, as I'm sure you're aware."

"I didn't fall off my horse, I don't fall...."

She smiled down at him. Or was she laughing? That charming smile had his hormones doing all sorts of double flips. *Hell.*

"I'm Molly, by the way. Dr Molly Simpson. I'll be taking care of you."

As she ran her soft hands over his chest, Kody winced. "Just as I thought – you might have broken a rib or two. Or maybe three." There was that cute smile again. Kody closed his eyes against the implications. "There will be no riding for you for quite some time," she said, moments before his eyes closed involuntarily.

"I really need to go home." Kody protested loudly when told he needed to stay in hospital another night.

Rory tried to calm him down. "There is no need to stress. We have it all under control." Kody glared at him, but Rory continued. "The horses have been taken care of, and I've sent one of my ranch hands over to make sure everything is as it should be. He'll be there until you're able to take over again."

Kody groaned.

It wasn't that he was worried about his ranch, although he was, it was more that he was sick of being in bed. He was bed ridden because of his concussion, and he was over it.

Very over it.

Although that cute little doctor was one consolation.

He shut his eyes against the thought. First of all, he was *not* interested in a relationship. The last one was an absolute disaster, and he didn't want to go there again.

Secondly, the cute little doctor, as he'd come to know her, wouldn't fraternize with her patients. She seemed pretty straight-laced, and with that would come some pretty decent ethics, he had no doubt.

"How are we today, Mr Callahan?" Was he dreaming, or was she really standing next to him?

"Kody," he said. "The name is Kody."

She touched him on the shoulder as though she was trying to wake him up. He opened his eyes from the thrill it caused and turned his head toward her. It still ached, but not as much as yesterday.

He lifted his hand to his stitched head. "You need to leave your stitches alone, Mr Callahan," she told him, completely ignoring his request to use his Christian name. "You'll end up dislodging the dressing." She sighed. "And then you'll be open to infection."

She glared at him as if to dare him to keep touching. "That would, of course, entail a longer hospital stay."

He squeezed his eyes tight. Now she was toying with him.

He heard his brother chuckle.

Okay, so he was a bad patient. He lived for the outdoors, hence owning a ranch, and spending most of his days on the back of a horse.

He looked up at her and smiled sweetly. "If I promise to behave, can I go home today?" He heard Rory snort with laughter.

She returned his smile, and busied herself checking him out all over, including his ribs. "That would be a no," she said as she walked away. "I'll see you in the morning."

11

He watched her walk away. Watched the wiggle of her cute little behind as she did so. He felt enamoured with this new lady doctor the hospital had employed.

"So much for laying on the charm," Rory told him, still chuckling.

"She's cute," Kody said, without thinking, and his brother stared at him with interest. Too much interest for Kody's liking.

He half sat up in the bed but lay down quickly as the dizziness overtook him.

"Molly told you about the dizziness, remember," Rory said, helping his brother to lay down again. "You whacked your head pretty bad and need to rest." He played with the pillows behind Kody's head. "Here, I can prop you up on some pillows if you like," he said, and Kody nodded his agreement.

It was going to be a long couple of days.

Kody lay back on the lounger overlooking the magnificent Montana Ranges.

He sat sipping coffee as he watched the sun rise. He breathed in the fresh country air. He listened to the tinkle of water from the nearby stream. And he watched the birds as they searched for worms in the garden.

Apart from the stitches in his head, and the pain it caused, he considered himself the luckiest man alive.

How many other men got to spend their days outdoors? How many of them got to make their own rules, and spend their time the way they wanted?

Sure, he had chores that needed to be done, horses to take to the sales yard, and fences to fix.

But he lived a happy life, even if he was alone. Despite telling his brothers the opposite, Kody *was* sometimes lonely. But he'd been bitten by not one but two women who had cheated on him. And he wasn't taking the chance again.

Despite what Rory said.

He wasn't looking for a partner just because he might get injured. That was never going to happen. If he found the right lady, then he might consider hooking up, but that wasn't on his radar right now.

The sting of breaking up was still fresh on his mind.

He took a big sip of his coffee and savoured the taste. The aroma hit his nose and boosted his taste buds. He was in heaven right now.

He suddenly felt weary. Placing his coffee mug on the side table, he closed his eyes – for just a few minutes.

Then he was dreaming.

The cute little doctor was standing over him, her face close to his.

She was touching his shoulder, and he could feel her warm breath as she leaned over him. He breathed deeply, and her fragrance hit his senses.

"Mr Callahan," Her sweet voice drifted over him. "Wake up, Mr Callahan!" Her voice was harsher now. As though her patience had run out.

He opened his eyes and the sunlight blocked his view. He shielded is eyes with his hand, and there she was.

She *was* standing over him. She was really there, not just a dream.

And she was close. So close – she was in kissing distance.

He shook the thought away and his head hurt like hell. "Ow!"

She stood up abruptly. "I've been trying to ring for hours, to make sure you were alright." She looked at him disapprovingly. "I was sure you'd gone out on your horse again." Then her face softened. "I was worried about you."

He sat up slowly to make sure the dizziness didn't hit him. This cruel creature would put him in hospital again if she knew he was still experiencing some giddiness, albeit when he moved too quickly. "Well, you don't have to worry, I'm okay," he told her, a little annoyed that she didn't trust him to do the right thing.

She stared into his eyes, as though doing so would reveal some medical mystery. "Are you experiencing any vertigo? Headaches? Pain?"

He let out a huge sigh. "I. Am. Okay." Since when did the hospital do house calls anyway? He stood and headed for the kitchen. "I'm putting the jug on. Want a cuppa?"

It was the least he could do, since she'd come all this way to check on him.

"Sure." The word came out of her mouth a little breathy.

He gestured for her to sit down at the table as he filled the jug. "Tea, coffee, whiskey?" The last came out on a laugh. He felt nervous around her, and his words were coming out all jumbled.

"Coffee. Thanks." She seemed a little more relaxed now. She smiled and her whole face lit up. And his heart skipped a beat.

Whoa! *What was that about?*

He set about normalizing the conversation. "Thanks for checking on me. I must have been in a deep sleep." He looked to the kitchen clock. 10am. "I closed my eyes for just a few minutes. At least I thought so, and that was at sunrise."

"You need the rest." She smiled tentatively. "The more you sleep, the better you will feel.

Concussion can be very dangerous if not treated properly."

He sat down opposite her, and suddenly felt awkward. Right then the jug screamed at him. He jumped up to make the drinks and went sideways.

He felt her hands steadying him, and then helping him into a chair. "Mr Callahan," He could hear the annoyance in her voice.

"Kody." He said it with conviction. "Please call me Kody. Mr Callahan was my father." The last sentence came out quietly. The boys had lost their parents a long time ago, but it still stung.

"Kody." He like the way his name rolled off her tongue, even if it was a little throaty. "You mustn't make sudden movements. You still have concussion, and it will take some time before it is completely gone."

He gazed up into her eyes as she leaned over him, still holding his shoulders. He moved closer to her face. His eyes bore into hers and only one thought crossed his mind. Kiss her.

Kiss her now!

He licked his lips. She licked hers too.

There was electricity between them. He felt it and was certain she felt it too. He lifted his hand and touched his fingers to her cheek.

"I, um," She backed off. Her fingers went to her lips as though he had actually kissed her. But he hadn't.

"Molly," he said, but realized he was being too intimate for the doctor/patient relationship. "Dr Simpson."

He wanted to ask her out. Wanted to get permission to kiss her. To hold her tight, and just be with her.

Instead he asked how she had her coffee.

She smiled, and he was sure she had read his thoughts. "White with two."

This was crazy. And totally irrational. She was his doctor. He was her patient. He could not be attracted to his doctor.

It was unethical. Illegal even.

"On second thoughts, I should go." She turned to leave but he grabbed her hand.

He didn't want her to leave. Her was enjoying her company, and he knew it was more than feeling a little lonely.

She looked into his face, then lifted her eyes to stare into his eyes. They slowly moved down his face until her eyes focused on his lips.

They stood face to face for what seemed forever. He licked his lips, then swallowed. He pulled his eyes away to break the trance they'd been in.

"Your coffee is ready," he said, as though nothing else had happened.

"I, I have to get back," she lied, but he ignored her lie, and handed her a mug of the steaming liquid.

"Would you like to take a walk in the garden?" Maybe she'd feel more comfortable out of the house? He could do with some fresh air, anyway.

"I really do have to go," she said. "I've been here far longer than I should have been." She sighed. Kody was good at reading people, and he was convinced she didn't want to leave.

"Come and see me at the hospital tomorrow," she said authoritatively. "For a check-up."

"Sorry, no can do," he told her cheekily. "My doctor says I can't drive." He chuckled, and she joined him, producing a delightful tinkling sound he was sure he'd never tire of hearing.

"Then I will do another house-call," she told him, wrapping her hands around the mug of coffee.

He grinned excitedly. He was going to see the cute little doctor again.

Molly picked up her doctor's bag and rushed toward her car.

Her heart fluttered with exhilaration.

He'd nearly kissed her – and what's more, she'd wanted him to. But he was her patient, and that wouldn't do. A doctor couldn't kiss her patient, even if he was the one instigating it.

She sat back in the driver's seat and strapped in, then took a deep breath. And another. And yet another.

What was she going to do? She'd felt something for Kody from the moment she'd seen him. She'd continued to call him Mr Callahan to try and keep some distance.

That worked out well. Not.

As she turned on the engine, she noticed him standing on the doorstep waving. She smiled and waved back.

What would he think if he knew it was her day off and she'd come on her own time? She didn't lie to him – she had been worried. When she couldn't get hold of him, she was worried out of her mind.

It was idiotic really. She'd only known him a matter of days. Heck, she'd only been at the hospital for about a week.

It was to be her sea change. To start her life over again.

Okay, time to face the truth. You were running away. But you can never run from yourself. Or your secrets.

As she drove from Kody's property, she admired the scenery. Took in the countryside. It really was beautiful out here. She was told it was quiet and secluded, but stunning at the same time.

She pulled to the side of the road. What the heck was she doing? She couldn't start a relationship. Not with anyone, but especially not with Kody. As much as she felt attracted to him, it was the last thing on her mind.

She had other responsibilities, and they had to come first. Like her hospital duties, and....

She'd worked so hard to become a doctor, despite all the odds. But she'd done it, and she wasn't prepared to throw it all away.

Maybe once she settled.

Who was she kidding? She would never be ready. Not ever.

She unstrapped her seatbelt and got out of her car to get some fresh air. Looking across at the Montana Ranges she knew she could easily spend the rest of her life here.

She also knew that could never happen.

Enough was enough.

Kody finished his coffee just as the sun finished rising.

He had his work boots on, and plonked his cowboy hat on his head. "Ow!" He quickly removed it.

No matter what the doc said, he'd put himself on light duties, and there wasn't a thing she could do about it.

He would muck out the stables first. Surely he couldn't do any further damage doing that simple task?

He walked into the stables and immediately the smell of horses and hay hit his senses. He'd missed coming in here every day. His hospital stay had put him out of action for only two days, but still, when it was something you loved...

Cracker came to greet him, hanging his head over the stall. "Hello fella. I've missed you," Kody told him, as the horse nickered into Kody's neck. He reached into his pocket and pulled out a carrot, which was quickly accepted and consumed.

The horse rubbed his head against Kody's shoulder. He'd apparently missed the contact with his owner too.

Opening the door to Cracker's stall, Kody grabbed the shovel, and began to muck out the stall.

21

Rory's stable hand had done a great job while he'd been recuperating, but he could do it himself now.

At least he though he could.

As he leaned forward to dig the shovel in the messed-up hay for the third time, pain ran through him. "What the hell...?" He hadn't expected that.

"Good question."

He spun around at the sound of Molly's voice, and nearly fell over. "What are you doing here so early?" He didn't mean for it to come out so snarky, but it did. He'd clear snapped at her.

He didn't think she'd even be out of bed yet, let alone do a house call before 7am.

"I, I came to check up on you. To..."

He interrupted her mid-sentence. "To make sure I was doing the right thing."

She looked annoyed. "I came to make sure you were okay. I knew you got up at sunrise, so I decided to come before I start my shift at 7am." She put her hands on her hips and glared at him.

He couldn't help himself, he stood there grinning. She looked so cute when she was mad.

"You know you could bust your stitches." She said it convincingly, and he wasn't certain if she was serious or not. Even mad, she was still attractive.

He was stuck where he stood. Kody couldn't move. He was so enamoured with her beauty and her charm. She was the most delightful woman he'd ever know. And he'd known a few.

"Tell me you haven't done anything yet." Her voice was hoarse, she was getting angrier the longer he stood without answering. "Kody. Really? You are going to just ignore me?"

He still held the shovel in mid-air. He shook his head to clear his head, but it only proved to cause more pain.

"Okay doc," he said. "You win." He left the stall and returned the shovel to the end of the stables.

He heard the breath leave her lungs as she breathed a sigh of relief.

He gazed into her almond shaped eyes. They were the most beautiful crystal blue eyes he'd ever seen. Still, he could be biased.

He stood there mesmerized for what seemed an eternity.

Cracker neighed and brought him out of his reverie. "Your eyes are beautiful?" He hadn't meant to say it out loud, but he was so enthralled by them, the words left his mouth before he could stop them.

His heart did a little dance at the tiny smile that appeared momentarily, then vanished just as quickly.

She watched him for mere moments, then brushed his words aside.

23

"Come outside, please. I need to check that wound." She turned tail and stormed out of the stables. She really was cute when she was mad.

Chapter Two

"You've busted a couple of stitches." She said it low-pan, as though she'd expected it. Which she had.

Kody had no idea his small amount of physical activity could do so much damage, she was pretty sure.

She felt mysteriously attracted to him but found him incredibly frustrating at times.

He lifted his hand to his head. "Seriously?"

She groaned. Just moments ago, he'd had that hand on a dirty shovel, and now he was reaching for his stitches.

Germ city.

"Yeah, Kody. Seriously." She sighed. She should be used to this sort of thing by now. Most people didn't understand the implications of putting dirty hands anywhere near open wounds.

She slammed her doctor's bag closed. "We'll have to go to the hospital and restitch your head." She looked at him pointedly. She didn't care if he realised she was annoyed.

Because she was annoyed!

And frustrated. Irritated. Disappointed. Plus a number of other things that she couldn't begin to verbalize right now for fear of upsetting her patient.

Of course, she couldn't say these things to him. It would be incredibly unprofessional of her. Instead she placed a clean dressing across his head and taped it down.

It would do until they arrived at the hospital.

The drive to the hospital was quiet. There was nothing much to say. He'd been an idiot, and he'd paid the price.

"Do you want to call one of your brothers?" she asked as they arrived. "You'll need someone to pick you up."

He shrugged. "I guess."

"I can't take you back. Sorry. I have to start my shift soon."

He called Jordon, who was a veterinarian, he'd told her. He'd be out and about, so it would probably be easier for him to come.

Kody sat quietly as she prepared to restitch his head. "I'm sorry," she said. "But I have to inject local anaesthetic again. That's the worst part."

"I guess that's what I get for being stupid, huh doc?"

"What the hell, bro? Even the animals don't bust their stitches," Jordon said. He hovered above Kody's head. "You did a good job of it."

Molly wrapped waterproof underlays all around his shoulder to stop his clothing being covered in blood.

Not that he was bleeding a lot, but he was bleeding. Better safe than sorry.

"I promise I won't do it again, Molly," he said, and Jordon raised his eyebrows. That was the moment Molly decided she needed to keep her distance from Kody. Her patient.

Her very appealing-to-her patient, but nonetheless, he was her patient.

Not that she was in a position to have a relationship. Her life had changed dramatically over the last year, hence her transfer to this small country hospital.

You could easily hide out here. Not many people even knew this town existed, let alone go looking for her here.

On the other hand, it could be easier to find someone in a small town – because every knew everyone else.

She sighed.

"All done." She busied herself packing up the equipment she'd used. "Please, *please*, do not muck out the stables again. Or do anything else that is likely to bust your stitches.

She turned to Jordon. "Can you and your brothers please keep an eye on this obstinate brother of yours? He is becoming the bane of my life."

With that she stared at Kody, smiled and touched his shoulder. "Please look after yourself," she said. Then turned and walked out the door.

"What's going on," Jordon asked.

Kody shrugged as they walked toward Jordon's truck. "Nothing's going on. What do you mean?"

It was obvious Jordon wasn't convinced. "I saw the way you looked at her. And the way she stared at you." He raised his eyebrows again. "There's definitely something between you two. Even blind Freddie would see it."

Kody grinned as he strapped himself into the passenger seat. "She is pretty cute, right?" He glanced across to his brother, then cleared his throat. "I mean, for a doctor, she's...."

"For a doctor?" Jordon glared at his brother. "So she can't be cute if she's a doctor? Hell, Kody!" He turned on the motor, quite obviously exasperated. "Anyway, I thought you'd given up women. Twice

28

bitten and all that. At least that's what you said after Annabelle."

Kody winced. "I never wanted to hear that name again. Besides, she's nothing like Annabelle. She's sweet, she's kind, she's beautiful. And she's...."

"Probably taken."

Kody looked up abruptly. His brother was probably right. It wasn't something he'd thought about. If she was all the things he thought she was, then she probably *did* have a boyfriend. Or a husband.

"Dang. I didn't even consider that." He sat brooding for the rest of the trip, not uttering a word to his inquisitive brother.

When he arrived home, Kody discovered one of Rory's stable hands mucking out the stable. "I had a go at that myself," he began to explain.

"Yeah, I heard," Pete answered. "I also heard you busted some stitches. Not cool, man. Just leave it to me until things are better."

Kody touched his hand to his newly bandaged head. "Guess so. Thanks Pete. It's appreciated." But Kody couldn't resist spending some time with Cracker.

He strolled toward Cracker's stall and called the horse over, enticing him with some apple. The horse whinnied, and Kody held out the apple for him to take.

Kody walked the few steps to the tack room and grabbed a halter. Since he was forbidden to ride, he'd decided to walk Cracker around the front paddock. That way they'd both get to have a bit of a stretch. Surely he couldn't bust his stitches again by walking?

Once the apple was consumed, which didn't take long at all, he gently put the halter over the horse's head. He opened the stall door, and the pair ambled toward the front paddock, Kody talking in low undertones.

It felt like forever since he'd been on this beautiful boy, but it was only a few days.

"What am I going to do, boy?" He rubbed his hand up and down Cracker's face. "What if she *is* taken? I don't think I could take it." They proceeded another hundred yards or so, then began walking in circles around the paddock.

"If she was taken, why would she be giving out signals like she is?" Now he was confused. Or maybe it was all one-sided. Was he reading into something that simply wasn't there?

His head hurt thinking about all the possibilities, but he needed to know. Was she as interested in him, as he was in her? Molly seemed to be interested. Hell, she'd nearly kissed him yesterday.

Okay, he nearly kissed her, but wasn't that the same thing? He lightly scratched his head, vowing not to do any more damage. *Was it the same thing?*

He pulled out another piece of apple and fed it to his equine companion, rubbing his fingers up the horse's face. "What do you think, Cracker? Does she like us?"

The horse neighed his agreement, and the pair continued on their walk around the paddock.

Not knowing was killing him, so Kody vowed to find out more about the mysterious Doctor Molly Simpson – one way or another.

He was developing a headache, so headed back to the stables. At least he didn't need much brain power to do that.

Molly shook her head.

What on earth was she thinking?

Every time she touched Kody Callahan, a thrill ran through her. Her heart hitched up, and it beat wildly. She even broke out in a sweat sometimes when he was near.

She felt like a love-struck teenager – thinking about him all the time. She'd even had to stop herself from calling him on several occasions.

When he'd moved close to her at his ranch-house, she was so tempted to connect with him, to kiss him, but backed off at the last moment.

She put her fingers to her lips.

Was this what it was like to fall in love, or was she simply overreacting?

It wasn't like she was looking for a companion, because she wasn't.

Her life was way too complicated to get involved with anyone. Even someone as appealing as Kody.

A chill went down her spine, and sadness overtook her. Of all the times in her life she had to meet him, it had to be now.

Why not a year ago?

She had already graduated medical school at that point and was fully qualified. She'd done her time working in general practice, and had a quiet life, albeit in another state. Sure, she worked long hours, as residents are compelled to do, and had very little time for a social life.

She would have found a way to work around it and was sure he would have too.

But now.... it was impossible.

Her life had change irreversibly. Now she had responsibilities. Now her life was massively different to what it was just one year ago.

And now she could no longer think about only herself.

She strolled out of the emergency department, ready to do her ward rounds. She swallowed hard and fought back tears. Why couldn't another doctor have been the one to tend to Kody when he was brought in?

If that had occurred, she wouldn't have to choose, and her heart would not be pulled in two like it was right now.

Kody was fed up being on light duties. Frustrated at not being able to ride. And downright bored.

He lay on his lounger drinking yet another mug of coffee and watching the sun rise. He counted down the minutes.

In just 372 minutes he would have his stitches removed.

And he would get to see Molly again.

He hadn't laid eyes on her for nearly two weeks.

Since he busted his stitches.

He wasn't willing to bust them all over again just to see her, so had no valid excuse to visit her at the hospital.

He downed the last dregs of his coffee and slammed the mug down on the table.

He pulled on his work boots and headed for stables. First job of the day – walk Cracker. He'd come to look forward to their walks each day but was biting at the bit to ride him.

He hadn't asked the question, so had no idea if he'd be allowed back on a horse at this point. He was frustrated with the situation but wasn't stupid. He wasn't going to take the risk of doing further damage.

"Hey fella." He called across to the horse as he headed for the tack room. After putting the halter over the horse's head, he offered a carrot. The pair then headed toward the front paddock.

It was boring walking Cracker every day; he'd much prefer to be riding him. This was the best-case scenario available right now, so he'd just have to live with it.

As they left the stables, he spoke to the horse quietly. "I can't wait to see her again, boy," he said. "I wonder if she's missed me as much as I've missed her."

Kody leaned in close to the horse, and Cracker neighed at him. As he nickered into his owner's neck, Kody looked up into the sky and revelled in the sight.

They did two more circuits of the paddock, then Kody took him back to the stables and gave the horse a good brush down, then fed him.

After making himself a good strong cup of coffee, Kody went to the office to do some administration work. He wasn't allowed to do anything physical, and he was behind with the paperwork. Besides, it would fill in quite a bit of time before he went to the hospital.

"Yo, Kody!" Chase stuck his head around the door to the office and looked inside. "You nearly ready? Don't want to be late for your appointment."

Kody sighed and stared at his brother. Did he really want to put himself through this torture? The stitches coming out weren't a bother; it was the torture of seeing Molly and not being able to touch her.

Not being able to be close with her.

Wanting so incredibly badly to kiss her.

"Don't stress, bro, you'll find a way." It was as though Chase could read his mind.

He stood and stretched himself out. He'd been sitting at that desk for over two hours. At least he'd caught up and didn't need to worry for a while.

He took a deep steadying breath. His brother stood silent, watching his every move. The corners of his mouth turned up slightly.

He was quiet on the trip to the hospital. It felt like hours instead of the forty minutes it took.

"Are you okay, bro?" Chase asked. "Other than the head, I mean? You're awful quiet, even for you."

"You wouldn't understand," he told his brother after a long moment of reflection.

"Try me." Chase took his eyes from the road momentarily to look at Kody. "What's the worst that could happen? I mean, I am your brother. I've been where you are now."

Kody frowned. "No you haven't. Not like this." He turned his head and stared out the window, sulking until they arrived at their destination.

As they strolled into the hospital, Kody heard the tinkling of laughter. He knew exactly who that sound belonged to.

He would know her voice anywhere. She was quietly confident, but authoritive at the same time. Not that he'd seen it for himself, but he was certain she would be playful when the situation presented itself.

He wanted so much to see it for himself.

As he walked toward the reception desk, he saw her. She was bent over, picking something up from the floor.

Her eyes met his and they both froze. Her face softened, and she smiled at him. But just as quickly, it hardened once more.

She quietly spoke to Natalie, the hospital receptionist, then motioned him into the treatment room.

"I'll wait out here," Chase told him as he sat on one of the waiting room chairs. Kody figured he was trying to give them a bit of privacy.

Kody sat down and waited. His heart raced, and he felt light-headed. He knew it wasn't from his injury, it was because of the conversation he intended to have with Dr Simpson. Molly.

He felt her first touch as she began to unravel the bandage from his head and watched as she threw it in the trash.

As she felt around the stitches, making sure they had all healed, he tried to slow his heartbeat, taking long, steadying breaths.

He closed his eyes, hoping it would help. It didn't.

"Right. So I'm about to remove the stitches," she said. "It won't hurt but might feel strange." She reached over and unwrapped the sterilized equipment she needed.

"Ready?"

He took a deep breath. "Ready as I'll ever be."

Kody sat quietly and calmly as each stitch came out. After she'd finished, Molly explained he still needed to be vigilant and look after himself, but he could start to do *some* physical work, but had to take it slowly.

"That's not a license to go hard and do anything you want," she reminded him. "Give yourself time to heal properly."

"Thanks Molly. I will," he promised as he stood.

But he got up too quickly and lost his balance. Molly grabbed his shoulders, and Kody felt the jolt run through him at lightning speed.

He looked up into her eyes, and discovered she was focused on him. She'd felt it too. He was certain of it.

She stood holding onto his shoulders for an eternity while they stood staring at each other. His heart beat ratched up a notch, until finally she turned her head away.

"Kody." He didn't know what to say. They were meant for each other. He knew it and she did too.

Soulmates.

He'd never felt like this before, and he could feel it in his heart.

At last she lifted her hands from his shoulders, then, without warning, placed one hand over his heart.

"Kody." She stood staring into his face while she continued to feel his heart beat. "There's so much I want to say to you," she said, barely audible. His heart began to beat more rapidly than before, and he could feel it pulsing in his ears.

Was she going to finally let him in? His heart raced with happiness. He couldn't wipe the smile off his face.

"I," She licked her lips and her eyes began to fill with tears. "I really want to be with you," she whispered so quietly he barely heard her.

He didn't understand the tears, happy maybe, but took that as her acceptance, and moved in toward her, his eyes focused on her lips. She licked her lips, and he found himself licking his too. As he moved closer, he gently brushed his lips against hers.

He relished being able to kiss her, to be near her, to feel her.

She closed her eyes and sighed against his cheek, and he knew she'd felt the same connection he had. His hand went up to touch her face, and she covered his hand with her own.

He wanted to be as close as he could to her, so put his arms around her and pulled her close.

She rested her head against his shoulder, and he heard her sigh again.

They were meant to be – he knew they were. She knew they were too, otherwise she wouldn't have reacted this way.

They stood together for a few minutes, then she suddenly pulled out of his grip.

She gazed deep into his eyes and spoke in a whisper. "I, can't. We can't." Her look was apologetic, as though she really wanted this, but found it to be an impossible task.

He lifted her hand and held it to his chest. "There's no reason...." he began, but she quickly interrupted him.

"Yes. Yes, there is." A tear rolled down her cheek, and he wiped it away with his fingers. "I can't do this."

He didn't think it possible, but his heart beat even fast. *What did she mean she couldn't do this?*

Was it because he was her patient? He could easily fix that – he'd request another doctor.

"Molly," his voice was so soft now, and he wasn't certain she even heard. "We can work through any problems there might...."

"This isn't fixable," she said sharply and pulled her hand out of his grip.

40

She stared at him sadly, then turned and walked away, her shoulders slumped.

He followed her to the doorway, then stood staring after her.

Chase met him at the door. "That doesn't look good, bro," he said quietly.

Kody shook his head, not sure he could find any words. "No," he finally said after long moments. "No, it's really not."

Chapter Three

Molly straightened her shoulders and walked away without looking back.

She didn't dare for fear she would give in to her feelings.

As she headed toward her office, she wiped at her cheeks. She'd made her decision, so why did it make her so unhappy?

Because you have feelings for him.

She shook her head against her errant thoughts. She'd only known Kody for a matter of weeks, but in that short time, he'd managed to get under her skin.

Like no one ever had before.

She'd dated several men over the years, but none of them had affected her the way Kody had. He had a laid-back attitude that rubbed off on her. When she was around him, she felt more relaxed, and didn't succumb to the hustle and bustle surrounding her.

And she had felt incredibly safe in his arms. That thought had her fighting back a sob.

She felt so drawn to him, it was uncanny. Even that first day in the emergency department –

there was something about him that made her feel connected with him.

She'd never experienced that before in her entire life.

Why did it have to happen now? Her life had changed irreversibly, and as much as she would like it to happen, Kody did not fit in to the plan.

She swiped at her tears and scurried toward her office, not wanting to be seen in this state.

"Dr Simpson?" She heard the words being called from behind her, but chose to ignore them, pretend she hadn't heard. Right now she wasn't in a fit state to talk to anyone.

The moment she entered her office, she slammed the door behind her. Molly sat at her desk, and put her hands to her face, then cried until there were no more tears.

"So what are you going to do about it?" Chase sat forward in his chair and pushed his brother for an answer. He could see how pained he was. Hell, he'd been there, he knew what it was like.

"I, I don't know," Kody whispered, his heartbreak evident. "Sometimes it seems to be one-sided – my side. And other times she reacts to me. I don't know where I stand."

43

As they sat in Kody's loungeroom sipping coffee, Chase goaded him. "You have to be more forthright. I know," he said. "I know that's not you. You're more the laid-back type, but if she's important to you, and I think she is, then you have to go after her." Chase sat back in his chair and stared at his brother, daring him to deny it all.

Kody sighed. "Honestly, I don't know what to do." He pushed his hat around his knees. "She seems to be hiding something, but I have no idea what it is." He stood and began pacing the floor as he ran his fingers through his hair.

Chase stared at him. "Hiding something? Are you sure?" This was new. Kody hadn't mentioned anything like this before.

"Yes. No." Kody was undecided. "No, I guess I'm not sure." He strode toward the chair and sat down once again.

Chase stared at him, mulling it all over in his mind. "Send her some flowers," he suddenly blurted out. "Women love flowers." He sat back in his chair grinning. "Yep, flowers will do the trick."

Kody ran his fingers across his unshaven chin. "You think?" He obviously wasn't convinced.

"Yes, sure. Definitely," Chase said, a little unsure himself, but at least it meant Kody was doing *something*, and not sitting around on his ass procrastinating.

44

Kody fiddled with his cell phone for a few minutes, then snatched up the telephone and dialled. "Hello? Yes, I'd like to send a dozen red roses, please."

Molly sat in her office doing paperwork. It was the last thing she wanted to do, but she was behind and had to tackle it sooner or later.

Sooner it was.

She rubbed her neck from the crick she had in it. She'd been sitting in one spot for far too long.

"Dr Simpson? Molly Simpson?" The stranger asked as he stood half turned in her office doorway.

"Yes?" She didn't have time for distractions. She needed to get through this annoying but necessary pile of forms before the day's end.

The stranger turned and walked into her office. He held a magnificent bouquet of red roses. The fragrance hit her before they were even close to her.

"Where would you like them, Ma'am," the delivery man asked, waiting for instructions.

Molly looked around the room, still startled by the surprise. "Ah, on the desk here will be fine, thank you."

As the man left the room, Molly breathed deeply, wallowing in the magnificent scent of the gorgeous flowers that sat right there on her desk.

She reached over and plucked the tiny card from between the stems. *Love will find a way.* She stared at the words hand-written on the card.

Tears threatened to well behind her eyes, but she fought them with all her might. *No! She would be strong. She'd resolved not to get involved, and nothing would change her mind.*

She read the card again and stared at the words: *Love will find a way.* He was right, she knew he was right, but not in this situation.

There was more at stake that he could ever imagine. She closed her eyes and imagined what it would be like to be held in Kody's arms every night. She felt herself sway at the thought.

Her heart was breaking in two. Despite only knowing him a very short time, she knew she was already falling in love. With a man she hardly knew.

She shook herself. That would never do. She couldn't bring a stranger......

She closed her eyes against the thought. She couldn't. She just couldn't. No matter how she felt, no matter what her heart was telling her. Her common sense was telling her otherwise.

"Tell me again why you complain every time another bunch of flowers arrive." Natalie was becoming more of a friend than just being the hospital receptionist.

Molly winced. "Because he's a patient?" She knew it was lame, and Natalie would too. But it was the best she had for now.

"That's easy fixed," Natalie said, brushing her excuse aside. "I'll allocate him to Dr Brown from now on. Besides, you signed off on him after the stitches came out." She eye-balled Molly, daring her to deny it. "He's no longer your patient. Next excuse?"

Natalie knew her too well. And she knew the patient/doctor relationship was an excuse as well. But as much as they had become friends, Natalie had never been to her house. Didn't know the full story, and hopefully wouldn't.

Molly didn't want to put her friend in danger. She liked her too much for that.

Every day flowers had arrived. Every day it had been a different romantic flower, today's flower was tulips. She'd already had roses, carnations, lilies, orchids, daisies, iris's and even sunflowers. She wondered what might be next.

What was she thinking? The procession of flowers had to stop!

As she leaned in to smell the tulips, Natalie looked across at her. "If I had a guy who sent flowers every day to get my attention, I'd surely be taking notice," she said. She frowned, as if she'd had a sudden thought.

"What's the real reason you keep backing off," Natalie asked. "He seems like a really nice guy."

Molly slid into her office chair and sighed. "He is," she said. "He really is. If I'd met him a year ago, I would have grabbed the opportunity with both hands." She put both her hands on the desk in front of her, as though trying to stop herself from fidgeting. "I can't stop thinking about him. Or about how one year has made such a huge difference to my life."

She suddenly gasped, realizing she'd said too much.

Natalie frowned. "What do you mean," she asked cautiously.

It was time. She needed to get it off her chest, but only if Natalie agreed to keep it to herself. "Grab a coffee," she commanded of her friend. "You're going to need it."

"Happy Valentine's Day, Dr Simpson." Natalie greeted Molly with a big grin on her face.

She'd had a sleepless night, thinking about Kody, and mulling things over in her mind, after baring her soul to Natalie.

She tried so hard to find a way to include him in her life. She really had.

But she couldn't.

Her life was busy enough here at the hospital, plus her responsibilities at home. She couldn't see how she could include a man in her life as well.

Add to that he had a big family. All of whom were capable of getting the word out.

She shook herself. It was never going to work.

"Happy Valentine's Day, Dr Simpson." The department secretary greeted her with a big smile. What was it with people today?

She gave her a friendly wave and strolled toward her office. At least they'd put a smile on her face and helped her out of her sulky mood.

After entering her office, she stood stock still, taking in the scene around her. Flowers were everywhere. On the desk, on the cupboards, the chairs, and even on the floor.

There was barely room to move.

She was stunned by the number of flowers confronting her. And she certainly was confronted – by the beauty of it all.

She breathed deeply. The aroma hit her nostrils and a vision of Kody came to her mind. It had to be him. No one else would go to this much trouble for *her.*

She stepped toward a bouquet on the desk and pulled out the small card.

Missing You.

She went to the next basket of flowers and pulled out the note. *Be Mine.*

And another said *I have feelings for you.* Yet another said *You are in my heart.*

Love conquers all.

Love is magic.

Love happens.

Two hearts entwined.

Love is not our choice, but our fate.

Feeling more than a little emotional, Molly gathered up all the note cards and held them to her heart.

"He really loves you." Natalie said, stepping toward her friend.

Molly looked at her and winced. "You know I can't be with him," she whispered. "As much as I'd like to"

"Molly," Natalie said quietly. "Just tell him. For God's sake, tell the man. He deserves to know."

She stood gazing at Molly for what seemed an eternity, then strolled out the door.

Molly picked up the telephone. What was she going to say to him? The phone rang for quite some time before answering.

"You've called..." She slammed down the phone. Why on earth was she calling him? That would just reinforce to him there was a chance for *them*. The two of them. Together. As a couple.

And there wasn't.

He'd had a hang up on his answering machine.

It had to be her. Apart from business calls, Kody rarely received phone calls.

That had to be a good sign, right? He smiled. Of course it was a good sign. She was buckling.

He'd sent flowers every day for two weeks in the lead up to today. Valentine's Day. It had cost a bomb, but he didn't care. She was more important to him than money.

What if his plan didn't work? What would he do then? Kody stiffened. He hadn't thought that far ahead.

But since she seemed to be caving, he would take advantage. He shaved and jumped in the

51

shower; since he'd been working around the ranch most of the day, he probably smelled like horse. He splashed on a little cologne and put on his best casual clothes.

He was ready for anything.

He sat in his truck in the hospital carpark, hands splayed across the steering wheel. What if she refused to go out with him? Or worse, she refused to see him?

Kody shook his head trying to clear the negative thoughts away. He couldn't let himself think like that. He had to think positive.

After waring with himself for over ten minutes, he finally got out of his truck. He walked the twenty or so steps toward the entrance, then paced back and forth, trying to build up the courage to walk through the door.

What if she says no, after everything he's done?

He straightened himself up, and stiffened his shoulders, then stormed in through the entrance.

The receptionist was beaming. "Good to see you, Mr Callahan," she said, with a grin that told him she knew more than a regular receptionist should. "I'm guessing you're here to see Dr Simpson."

It wasn't a question. She was quite assertive.

Kody felt himself relaxing. Or was he backing away? No, never!

She leaned forward and whispered so only he could hear. "The flowers are beautiful," she said. "Don't take *no* for an answer."

"I don't intend to," he whispered back.

She stood taller and nodded. "Good," she said. "Follow me."

The walk to Molly's office seemed to take forever, as though he was walking to an execution. The longer he walked, the more his heart pounded. He wiped the sweat from above his lip.

"I'm Natalie, by the way," she told him. "Don't stress, it will be okay." She put her hand to his shoulder, as if to reassure him further.

"I sure hope so, Natalie," he said as they came to an office that had Molly's name on the door.

Natalie tapped lightly, then opened the door. "You have a visitor," she said, then winked at Kody and pushed him inside. She shut the door behind her.

Molly glanced up from what she was doing. Obviously startled by the interruption. "Kody," she said. "I didn't expect to see you today."

"And yet, here I am," he said, not sure what else to say.

He looked around the room, taking in the baskets of flowers he'd sent. They were pretty, really pretty. And they smelled so nice too.

53

She indicated for him to sit down, and he quickly sat before she changed her mind. "How have you been, Molly?" He genuinely wanted to know. He'd really missed her.

"Fine. And you?" she asked, probably out of good manners. "How is your head now?"

"It's fine. I'm fine too," he said, feeling rather awkward at this point. "Have dinner with me," he blurted out, not wanting to be so forthcoming, but in hindsight realizing it was the best way to be given the circumstances.

She sat back in her chair and brushed some hair off her face. "I'm tied up here," she said, waving her hands above the papers laying on her desk.

He was disappointed, he wouldn't kid himself. But he knew it wouldn't be easy. He'd spent literally weeks trying to get close to this stubborn woman, and the fact she hadn't sent his flowers back, spoke volumes to him.

He leaned in as close to her as he could get. He stared at her over the desk. It was all he could do to stop himself from jumping over the top and kissing her senseless. "You have to eat sometime," he said instead. Then leaned back in the chair and crossed his arms. "I can wait until you're ready."

He stared her down, daring her to say no.

"Kody, I..."

He stopped himself from sighing out loud. He knew this could happen. "I'm not taking no for an answer," he said assertively. "There is no reason for you not to,"

She interrupted him before he could finish. "There is," she said quietly. "I should have told you a long time ago."

He sat stunned. What could be so terrible they couldn't date?

"I'm so sorry," she whispered. He could see the tears welling up in her eyes. He couldn't cope when women cried, but for both their sakes, he sat glued to the seat.

"Nothing is that bad," he told her, hoping he was right.

She sat taller in her seat and braced her shoulders. "I have..." At that very moment her cell phone rang. "Sorry, I have to take this," she told him, obviously distressed about the interruption.

"Simpson." She listened intently, then stood to leave. "I'm sorry, I have to go," she said, ushering him out the door. "It's your sister-in-law, she's in labor," she finished, rushing off.

Kody rushed out to the waiting room, where Rory stood bewildered.

"Where's Missy," Kody asked. "Shouldn't you be with her?" he asked, touching Rory's shoulder when he didn't get an answer. "Where is Missy?"

Kody guided his brother to one of the waiting room chairs. "You do know you should be with her, right?"

Rory turned to look at him, still feeling dazed. "It wasn't meant to happen yet," he said, feeling quite worried.

Jordon strolled through the door, overhearing the conversation. "She's only a few days early. It's nothing to worry about."

"She, her," Rory was tongue-tied.

"Her water broke," Molly said for him as she entered the waiting room. "It's nothing to worry about. Okay Rory, you can come in now."

He followed the doctor into the birthing room. Missy sat up in bed, propped by several pillows. "You look pale," he said, fluffing the pillows up for her.

She glared at him. "You try being in labor and see how you feel," she snapped at him. *Oh boy. And this was just the beginning.*

Rory watched as Molly went to one of the cupboards. "Here's a robe," she said. "Put this on and start walking."

"It will help bring the labor on quicker," she said, answering Rory's silent question. "You need to stay with her, dad," Molly said.

Dad? He liked the sound of that.

"We don't like our pregnant ladies falling over." He nodded but didn't answer. "Got it?"

"Yes, Ma'am," he finally responded. It was finally all happening. After all these months of waiting for their precious cargo, it was finally all happening.

Rory took a deep breath. Missy slapped him on the arm. "I'm the one who needs to breathe, not you," she said, chuckling. She looked into his eyes and Rory melted.

He loved this beautiful woman more than he thought it was ever possible to love some one. And now she was having his baby.

Right now! Holy heck!

He grabbed hold of Missy. "We're having a baby," he said, incredulous.

She laughed with that lovely tinkle he loved to hear. "Yes, we are," she said. "Very soon."

Rory helped her out of bed and into the soft terry robe. His hands melded around her very swollen belly, and he kissed her gently.

"Mommy and daddy are ready and waiting for you Chloe," he said as he kissed Missy's belly.

Chapter Four

The three brothers were pacing the floor in the waiting room, along with their partners, when Rory returned some hours later.

"It's a girl!" he announced proudly. "Chloe Melissa. Don't know how much she weighs yet, but Chloe is fine, and Missy is exhausted." He grinned broadly.

Jordon, Kody, and Chase slapped him on the back, and hugged him tight. Grace and Isabella, Jordon and Chase's partners, hugged each other and wiped tears from their eyes.

"I'll bet she's beautiful," Grace declared, as she walked toward Rory.

As she wrapped her arms around him, Rory told her she certainly was. "More beautiful than you can imagine," he said proudly.

Molly entered the waiting room and spoke quietly to Rory. "Missy is asking for you," she said. "Don't stay too long, she needs to rest."

And that was that. Rory left to go to Missy, as it should be. Kody looked across the room to see Molly staring at him.

"Everything went fine," she told the room of Callahan's. Both mother and baby need some rest, so maybe you could all come back tomorrow."

Kody admitted he was disappointed. He'd hoped to see his new baby niece today, and now that wasn't going to happen.

But he understood. Having a baby was a big effort, and Missy would be tired. Hell, she'd be exhausted.

His shoulders dropped, and he began to walk away, certain Molly would also need to rest. She was after all, Missy's doctor.

"Kody," she said quietly so no one else would hear. "I know we didn't finish our conversation."

He looked at her sadly. "There's always tomorrow," he said. Resigned to the fact they wouldn't get to go for their Valentine's Day dinner.

She stood staring at him, not saying a word, and his heart pounded. *What was she thinking?*

He turned toward his brothers who were about to leave the hospital, all of them elated at the new family member. He felt the same, but felt he wasn't giving it his full attention since he was so focused on Molly right now.

She put her hands to her hips and tapped her foot. "So I don't get to eat after all?" she said matter of factly. Her eyes bore into him, and heart beating rapidly, he strolled to her side and took her hand.

59

"You certainly do," he said happily. "You most certainly do." He couldn't wipe the grin off his face.

"I'm on call tonight," she said as she perused the menu. It was a risk Kody was willing to take. He was just grateful he finally got to sit down and talk to her face to face.

There was an Asian restaurant within walking distance of the hospital, so they opted for that. At least that way Molly could get back to the hospital quickly if required.

No matter how many times he read the menu, or more accurately, stared at the menu, nothing seemed to stick in his mind. His thoughts were elsewhere.

What was so important that Molly felt obligated to tell him?

He gazed at her over the menu. Her eyes were darting all over the place. She suddenly looked up at him. "What?" she demanded.

"Oh, nothing," he said casually. Kody reached across the table and touched her free hand. "I'm so pleased we could still go out tonight," he said quietly. "It's like a date."

She glanced across at him. "*Like* a date?" She looked amused. "So if this is not an actual date, what is it?"

For a grown man in his thirties, he sure was stupid sometimes. "I meant," he fumbled, losing his train of thought. "Of course it's a real date, but I wasn't sure if you..."

Molly quickly interrupted, laughing as she did. "I'm pulling your leg. I do see it as a date. Don't you?" Now she sounded a little worried.

He was about to answer when the waiter approached their table, so he snatched his hand away and nodded instead. Molly grinned at him, and he breathed a sigh of relief.

They placed their orders, and the waiter left to get their beverages.

He slid his hand across to hers again.

"Your wine, Sir, and your water, Madam."

It seemed they were destined to be interrupted all evening. Kody decided not to pursue where they left off earlier in Molly's office until after dinner.

"Tell me about yourself," Kody said, wanting to break the silence.

Molly braced herself by straightening her back and shoulders. "There's not a lot to tell," she answered. "I worked hard to become a doctor. Put myself through medical school, working part-time and still managing to study." She took a deep breath.

"It was hard," she said. "Really hard. Then I had to do my post-grad work before I was fully qualified." She waved her hands around and suddenly went silent before continuing a minute or so later.

"And here I am today," she said. "Oh, I've been qualified for a couple of years now," she added quickly.

Kody smiled. She was a hard worker, just like him.

He reached across the table to touch her hand, but the food arrived, and he snatched it back into his lap.

She gave him a lopsided grin, as though commiserating with him. "This smells amazing," she said, leaning in to get a better smell of the wonderful aroma.

He leaned in too. "It sure does. Well, go on. Eat it while it's hot." Kody picked up the chopsticks and tried for a few minutes to master them. "Waiter," he called, indicating to the server. "Can we have a couple of forks please?"

"What?" he said, noticing Molly laughing behind her hands. "They're hard to use," he said as Molly picked up her chopsticks and began to eat without issue. He watched as she giggled while she ate.

She looked so beautiful when she laughed. Hell, she looked beautiful all the time.

He reached across and brushed a thumb across her cheek. "Molly," he said quietly, gazing directly into her mesmerising blue eyes.

"We should eat," she said bluntly. "I'm on call, remember. I may have to leave at any moment."

He nodded and reluctantly removed his hand. "Sure," he said, and turned to his food, not really tasting it, wondering what it was she wanted to tell him.

"That was an amazing meal," she said, finishing off the last mouthful of banana fritters and ice cream.

Coffee was left on the table, and the waiter made himself scarce. Almost as though he knew they needed to talk privately.

Kody wiped his mouth with the linen napkin. "I've only been here once before, but the food was every bit as good as it was tonight," he said, hoping Molly would open up to him soon. After all, she was still on call, and could get a phone call at any moment. They'd been lucky up until now.

He watched her as he sipped his coffee, and she glanced over the rim at him. "Molly..."

"Kody."

63

They spoke at almost the same time.

"Kody, I really have to tell you this. It's important," she said. "Otherwise our relationship is based on a lie."

It got more and more interesting as time went on. And curious.

"But I'm not sure *here* is the right place for this conversation."

He covered her hand with his, not saying a word. He didn't want to interrupt her, as had been done all evening, by various means.

"Kody, I....." Her cell phone rang. "Damn it!" He could see she was frustrated, and annoyed, but she was on call. There was nothing they could do about it.

"Sorry," she said, genuinely regretting the disruption. "Another baby has decided to arrive." She bit her lip, full of regret.

"Don't stress it," he said, helping her off her chair. "There's always tomorrow."

He might have sounded nonchalant, but inside his gut was churning. What was so important that she was stressing so much about telling him? And why didn't she feel comfortable doing it there in the restaurant?

He certainly wasn't going to get any answers tonight.

Kody helped Molly into her jacket, paid the bill, then walked her back to the hospital. Urging her into a semi-dark corner outside the entrance, he pulled her close and kissed her gently on the lips.

He could still taste the banana fritter from desert. It was sweet, like Molly. He cupped her face with his hands and looked into her eyes. "Molly, I know we haven't known each other that long," he said. "Or had a lot of contact, but I think I'm falling in love with you," he said quietly. So quietly he almost didn't hear it himself.

She leaned into him and rested her head on his shoulder. "Kody," she whispered. "I have feelings for you too." She sighed heavily. "I honestly wish I wasn't on call tonight. There's so much we need to talk about. That.... that I need to tell you."

He pushed back and looked into her eyes. "Tell me now," he said, voice cracking with anticipation.

"I, I can't," she said, as she pulled away and quickly strode into the hospital.

He stared after her, wondering what on earth had her so scared.

Kody tossed and turned all night, thinking about Molly and what she wanted to tell him.

He understood she was on call, he really did, but why did she have to get called back to the hospital at that precise moment?

Another minute or two and she would have revealed what was bothering her. Wouldn't she?

He lay in bed staring at the ceiling. After Annabelle, he'd sworn off women forever. He now knew that it only needed the right woman to come along for him to change his mind.

And indeed, she had. Molly was the right woman. He was certain of it.

He glanced across at the clock, which stood out against the blackened room.

3am.

He pulled the covers further up the bed, and wrapped himself in them, closing his eyes against the glare of the clock.

"Damn it, Molly!" he shouted to the empty room. "Why did you have to be my doctor?" He was certain things would be different now if she hadn't attended to him in emergency that day.

But then again, they may never had met.

He wondered again what she was so desperate to tell him. Perhaps she was already married? The thought left him as quickly as it had arrived.

She would have told him from the start. She was honest to the core.

He would call her now and find out. The glare of light hit him in the face, and he glanced at the clock again.

Perhaps not.

He snuggled down and tried to get back to sleep, but his head hurt from worrying. He rolled out of bed and sat on the edge for what seemed ages, then pulled on his jeans, and finally headed to the kitchen where he made coffee.

Lots of it.

He was convinced he wouldn't get back to sleep again and decided to tackle some of the overdue paperwork.

Kody awoke with a start.

After almost three hours of paperwork he'd retreated to the outside lounger to watch the sun rise. His favourite thing to do.

He was somewhat disoriented, and looked around, realizing where he was. But he couldn't seem to stop the ringing in his head.

As he shook his head to clear away the cobwebs, he it finally dawned on him the telephone was ringing.

Molly.

She was the only one game enough to call him at that hour of the day. He ran to the kitchen and pounced on the phone, but it was too late. She'd hung up.

The little red light showed on the machine, so he knew she was leaving a message. He was impatient to listen but had to wait until the call was fully recorded.

He stood tapping one foot, sighing as he did so.

"Come one. Hurry up," he told the inanimate object, as though it could hear him.

Finally the light went out and he could listen.

"It's Molly," her sweet voice said. "I, um." There was a slight pause before she continued. "I had hoped to catch you, but obviously I didn't. I'm really sorry about last night."

Yeah, Kody was too. His mind went back to their kiss. If she hadn't needed to rush off and deliver a baby, it could have been so much more.

He was so busy with his own thoughts, he missed the end of the message and had to replay it.

"I'm really sorry about last night. I finish at four today, and if you're free, there's something I want to show you."

Was she kidding? He would make himself available, even if it meant moving heaven and earth.

With renewed vigour, he organised himself for work. First off, feed Cracker. He'd have another coffee while the horse ate, and then the two would go and check the boundary fences.

He stood tall as he wondered exactly what it was she wanted to show him. He also questioned if she had any intention of finally telling him what she deemed so important.

If he got to learn at least one of these things, he'd be a very happy man.

At least today there should be no interruptions.

And of course, spending time with Molly was always a bonus.

He held tightly to the reins and urged the horse forward. Not far to go now.

He needed to arrive back at the homestead at 2.45pm.

Time enough for a shower and to make himself presentable before driving to the hospital which was about forty minutes away.

After removing the saddle, Kody offered Cracker some water, which he gladly accepted. Despite being anxious about this afternoon's rendezvous, he cared for Cracker in the way he deserved to be treated.

The next fifteen minutes were spent walking around the front paddock, allowing Cracker to cool down after their long and vigorous ride.

Finally, he was treated to a brush down and returned to his stall.

Now it was time to pamper himself. Right now he smelled like the devil. There was no way he would go anywhere near Molly smelling this bad!

The shower was bliss. The steaming hot water rolled over his body, taking away all the aches and pains from the day's work.

Fixing fences was an ongoing job, but if he wanted to keep his stock inside his property, it had to be done.

Adding shampoo to his hair triggered unwanted thoughts. Fantasies of Molly running her hands thought his thick brown hair as she kissed him ever so lightly. Teasing him endlessly, until finally...

He shook himself, trying to erase the thoughts. All they did was awaken urges he didn't want to contemplate. He wanted to get to know Molly much more before they even thought about taking the plunge.

As he continued to wash himself, the combination of hot water and slippery soap was titillating. Especially as he began to wash his private parts.

His thoughts were going places he didn't want to go, so he turned off the hot water completely, leaving him with an icy cold shower.

"Brrrrrrrrrrrrrrrrr!"

He finally turned off the water and stepped onto the bath mat to dry himself. The fluffy white towel had him thinking about being wrapped in Molly's arms.

Stop it!

Man oh man. He had it bad. The sooner he arrived in town and met with her, the better.

His mind was telling him to step away – he was too heavily involved already – but his heart was saying meeting her was the best thing that had ever happened to him.

Chapter Five

He paced outside the hospital entrance waiting for Molly to appear.

Despite everything, he'd arrived fifteen minutes early. He wasn't a particularly patient man at any time, but the events of the past few days had him extremely nervous.

At 4.01 precisely, she stepped outside. His heart did a little flutter at the sight of her. "I missed you," he said, stepping forward and wrapping his arms around her. She stiffened, and he wondered why.

As he kissed her forehead, she relaxed into him, and leaned her head on his shoulder. He pulled her closer to him.

"I missed you too," she said quietly. "And I can't apologize more about last night, but when you're the doctor on call..."

He interrupted her mid-sentence. "I understand, I really do," he said. "Although it is getting a little stale. This being disturbed all the time."

She put her arms up his back, then pulled back to look into his face.

"I'm sorry," she said, and looked sincere. "No interruptions today, I promise," she said, stone-faced. "My shift is finished, and I'm not on call." He stared at her, not sure whether to believe it or not. "I promise," she said more forcibly.

"Okay," she said. "Let's not put this off any longer."

He looked at her quizzically, then followed her lead.

"We're going to my apartment," she said. "There's something I have to show you."

He nodded but didn't say a word. Didn't dare in case he jinxed them. His heart beat wildly, more intrigued by the moment.

"We can walk, it's only two blocks away." She took his hand, and his heart skipped a beat.

"I really am sorry," she said softly.

"You have nothing to be sorry for," he said, certain it was true.

She squeezed his hand as they continued to walk. "You can decide that later," she said.

Every step he took was another step closer to finding out what she'd been hiding all this time. As much as he wanted to know, needed to know, a feeling of dread came over him.

"This is it," she said, standing in front of an apartment block.

As they walked down the hallway, every step Kody took echoed in his head. Every step seemed like a death knell, not knowing what was about to transpire.

But every step also brought him closer to the truth.

She pulled out her keys and opened the door. As they stood in the entrance, he looked around. He thought about how confined it seemed compared to the big open spaces of his ranch. There was no way he could live here.

As he continued to peruse the room, something was amiss. He couldn't put his finger on it, but there was something. It was eating away at him.

Then he realized. There were toys in the apartment.

For a moment or two he stood stunned. She was a mother? She had a kid? That was the big secret? He breathed a huge sigh of relief as he stood staring at the toys.

For a while there, he'd thought it was something dreadful that meant they couldn't be together.

"Take a seat," she said, indicating for him to sit in a recliner chair, not realizing he'd figured it out. "I'll be back in a moment."

A young woman came out of the kitchen as Molly went into another room. "Hi, I'm Karen," she said.

Kody stood. "Pleased to meet you," he said, extending his hand. "I'm Kody."

"Yes, I know," she said, then sat down on another chair.

His interest was really peaked now. Who was this Karen person, and why was she here?

He felt Molly's presence before he saw or heard her.

"Kody," she said. "There's someone I'd like you to meet." She stood in the doorway of one of the rooms and appeared to be trying to coax someone out.

I'd like you to meet, Madison." she said when the little one finally appeared. The little girl smiled at him tentatively and looked like she might even burst into tears.

She stayed close to Molly and held tightly to her hand as she walked slowly toward him.

"Hello, Madison," he said through the fog of his brain. He did his best to smile but didn't want to scare the kid.

Molly came to sit beside him. "Madison is a big three-year-old." She grinned at the child who smiled for the first time.

75

She had a sweet smile, and Kody was endeared by her.

"Hello," she said coyly, then moved forward and wrapped her little arms around him in a big hug. Kody felt a huge lump at the back of his throat, making it hard to swallow. He slowly put his arms up and wrapped them gently around the toddler.

He looked at Molly over Madison's shoulder and grinned. He felt like a big goof-ball right now.

Madison suddenly dropped her hands. "Can I go and play with Karen now," she asked.

Molly looked long and hard into his eyes, then turned back to the child. "Sure, honey. Off you go."

He leaned back in his chair, highly relieved. "Madison is the big secret," he said, barely audible. "She's very cute."

Kody reached across and took her hand. "You must have been young when you had her," he said, leaning closer to Molly.

"What? No!" she told him. "Madison is not my daughter, you big dope. She's my niece."

Now Kody was confused. If she wasn't Molly's child, why was she living with Molly?

"I can see you're confused, but we can't discuss it here." He nodded knowing she was right. "Anywhere in public isn't really suitable unless it's quiet. And I don't want to go back to the hospital for fear of being dragged into something."

"We can go to my place," he offered. "It's quiet at the ranch, with little chance of being disturbed."

Molly looked relieved. "That's a great idea," she said. "Let me get changed first, and then we can go."

As she left the room, Kody sat back in the chair. His head was full of scenarios now. Something seemed terribly amiss, but he wasn't sure what.

They went to the ranch in Kody's truck. That way, he'd told her, they could have dinner later. Of course, young Madison was welcome to come along too.

Molly had frowned at the suggestion, and he wasn't sure why, but she came in his truck anyhow.

She didn't say a word on the trip home, so he didn't interrupt her thoughts.

He made a fresh pot of coffee when they arrived. He figured the way she was so mysterious about the whole situation, he might need it.

And she might need it for courage.

They sat outside, in the fresh air. The fact it was a little less formal out there should also help. He handed her the coffee and sat down with his own.

"Molly,"

"Kody..."

They spoke at the same time. "You first," she said.

He took a long sip of the hot brew. "You don't have to tell me anything, if you don't want to," he told her in a soft voice.

She stared at him momentarily, then said "Yes. I do." She brushed the hair from her face and looked down into her lap. "Madison is my sister's child."

He didn't say a word, for fear the interruption would upset her.

"My dead sister," she added and looked up at him. "She was a drug addict." She paused, and he wondered if she was waiting to see his reaction.

He nodded. "I'm very sorry," he said quietly.

She waved a hand across in front of herself. "Water under the bridge. Madison is all I care about now. Caring for her and protecting her." She sighed and sat back in her seat, taking a big mouthful of coffee as if it might sustain what she had to say next.

"Her father is still alive, and trying to get her back," she said quietly. So quietly that Kody had to lean in close to hear what she was saying.

She looked up at him, determination in her eyes. "He's a drug addict too," she said, barely breathing as she spoke. "I have full custody, but he won't accept it, and is trying to get her back." A tear rolled down her face, and Kody brushed it away with his fingers.

He put his coffee down and took her cup as well, then pulled her into his arms. "Oh Molly, you poor thing," he said. "Keeping this all bottled up and having to deal with so much on your own." He stroked her hair as he held her tight. "Why didn't you just tell me in the beginning?"

She pulled out of his arms and stared at him for what seemed hours. "Because I was afraid you wouldn't want me."

He pulled her back into his arms again and held her tight. "Molly," he said. "That would never have happened." He felt her sobbing against his shoulder. "I love you, and nothing as tiny as a three-year-old would stop that."

She pulled back and looked at him. "Really?"

"Yeah, really." They stared at each other for a heartbeat, then Kody thought of his brother. "Let's get Chase onto this," he said. "You can't keep Madison locked up forever."

She shook her head. "I, I can't risk her being outside," she said. "He might find her. And I couldn't bear to lose her." She shook her head as though chasing those demons away. "Not to mention what would happen if she lived with her father. Scum that he is. If it wasn't for him, my sister would still be alive."

Kody didn't interrupt but let her get it all off her chest. "She didn't do drugs until he came along."

He stood, and she followed suit. He wrapped her a big bear hug and held her tight until she stopped shaking. "I'll call Chase, and get some fresh coffee," he said. "You need it, I think."

She followed him inside and waited while he made the call to Chase. "He'll be over shortly," he told her.

He gave her a tour of the house while they waited. It wasn't huge but wasn't tiny either. Kody had built it with the future in mind. He'd hoped that one day he'd have a family, but it wasn't to be.

"I love the fresh air out here," Molly told him as they stood outside waiting for Chase to arrive. "You have such a beautiful view here. The mountains, the paddocks, everything.

He took her hand and led her to the stables. "Meet Cracker," he said, handing her a piece of carrot. "He won't bite and loves carrots." He smiled at her, and for the first time in a few hours, he felt relaxed and happy.

80

"Is this the horse that threw you," she asked suspiciously.

"Yes," he answered. "No! Cracker wouldn't throw me off his back. I have no idea what happened, but it wouldn't have been his fault."

"Helloooooo." Chase's voice echoed through the stables. "I figured you must be out here," he said, then suddenly looked officious.

Molly stiffened next to him, and Kody put his hand to her back. "It will be okay," he whispered in her ear, then led her back to the house with a bigger feeling of dread than he'd had earlier that day.

Deputy Chris Dolan was waiting at Kody's front door.

He often accompanied Chase on official business and was the sheriff's right-hand man. "Kody," he said. "Ma'am." He lifted his hat as he acknowledged Molly. The deputy had his pen poised over his notebook.

Kody indicated for them to all sit down. "I have a fresh pot of coffee brewing," he said. "Any takers?"

Three hands went up, and Kody busied himself with refreshments while the sheriff and his deputy spoke to Molly.

He stood at the kitchen window and contemplated his life with Molly and Madison in it.

81

He'd built this house with a family in mind, but never contemplated this situation.

He took a deep breath. He was assuming too much. Molly may never want to live here with him.

Unless they could do something about the dead-beat father, his idea of the three of them as a family would never come to fruition anyway.

He shook himself, trying to chase the negative thoughts away, then poured the coffees and carried them outside.

"I believe we have enough information to sort this out," he heard Chase say as he stepped outside. "But it may take some time," he said. "I suggest you keep the little one hidden for now. I'll get back to you as soon as I know something."

He took his coffee and sat back to enjoy it. "Thanks Bro," he said. "At least you have decent coffee. The station coffee is horrific."

"Sure is," Chris added. "Undrinkable even."

Chase laughed. "Which is why I frequent Aunt Lizzie's Kitchen. Now *that* woman knows how to make coffee!"

Chase and Deputy Chris had left, leaving them alone.

They sat in silence for a few minutes, until Kody broke the awkward silence. "Have we got time for a walk," he asked. "Or do we have to rush off?"

Molly checked her watch. "Are we still doing dinner? I'll have to feed Madison first. Or I could get Karen to do it."

Kody stared at her. "Who is this Karen, anyway?" he asked, his curiosity getting the better of him.

She laughed, and the happy sound warmed him. "She's Maddison's nanny. A live-in nanny, since I work all kinds of odd hours." She watched as she waited for his reaction.

He shrugged. "I guess being a single parent brings its challenges," he said. "I can't imagine how hard it's been for you."

He stood to collect all the coffee mugs, and Molly stood too. She stepped toward him, looking so forlorn that Kody moved toward her and wrapped his arms around her. "I love your big bear hugs," she said quietly. "They are so.... comforting." She rested her head against his shoulder and let him take her weight.

As he brought his hand up her back, he felt her shift her weight to bring her closer still. He revelled in her nearness – he could stand like that all day. He felt so enthralled by this woman, and he wanted more of her. Her and Madison.

He certainly hoped Chase could sort this mess out. The sooner he managed to do that, the better he would get to know Molly, as well as her little niece.

They stood like that for some minutes until Molly broke the spell he was under. "Can we go for that walk? I think I need some fresh air to clear my head."

She pulled back and looked up into his eyes, then slowly moved toward his face. Kody looked down into her mesmerizing blue eyes. He felt drawn to them, to her, and moved toward her lips.

"I'm going to kiss you," he whispered. "Is that okay?" He waited mid-way for her response.

Her eyebrows shot up. "Don't ask to kiss me, just do it, silly!"

As he moved toward her, he could smell the light fragrance of lavender. It wasn't overpowering and was definitely the essence of Molly. Every time they'd met, her lavender fragrance was one of the first things he noticed.

He lightly brushed his lips against hers, then leaned down to her neck. He brushed light kisses all the way down, then worked his way back up again.

"Kody," she whispered breathlessly. "Just kiss me for goodness sakes." She moved her head so he had no choice.

84

He leaned into her, and claimed her lips, covering her mouth with his. He'd been deprived of a real kiss until now, and it had proved to make him only want her more.

Molly melted into his arms, and returned the kiss, pushing her tongue into his mouth. He savoured it and responded with his tongue.

"Molly," he whispered hoarsely. "We need to stop, otherwise it might go further." He pulled back and looked into her eyes. He saw the need there but knew this was not the time. He would not take advantage of her during this difficult time.

"Today is not a good day, after all you've been through," he said, pulling out of her arms. "Let's go for that walk. I think the fresh air could do us both some good." He winked, then guided Molly toward his garden. It was a mixture of flowers and vegetables, and was impressive, if he did say so himself.

"You did all this?" Molly's eyes were wide.

"Yeah, over the years," he said. "Bit by bit. It supplies most of my vegetables. So much nicer than bought stuff," he told her.

"Over there is the chook pen," he said. "I get six or eight eggs a day from that lot, most of which I don't use. When I have enough I hand them out to my brothers. No point wasting them." He shrugged.

"I would love fresh eggs to bake with," she said excitedly.

He smiled. "You're welcome to them."

Molly shook her head frantically. "No, no," she said. "I wasn't implying...."

But he stopped her protests with a kiss, putting his hand to the back of her head. "Molly," he said softly. "Take some eggs. I have plenty."

"But," He pulled her close again, and was lost in her. When he finally pulled back, and opened his eyes, her eyes were bright with passion, and the tension had left her face.

"Oh heck," she exclaimed. "We have to go. Look at the time!"

It was well after five, and they had that long drive back to Bolton, where Molly lived.

Kody scrambled toward the hen house, then went in, basket in hand. She watched in wonder as he filled the basket with eggs before coming back out.

"Omelettes for breakfast?" he asked, laughing and handing them over.

"I, I can't," she said.

He leaned forward and planted a kiss on her forehead. "You can, and you will," he said. "I honestly can't use them."

Molly stretched herself out and gazed around her. "Madison would love it here. So much room for her to run around. Not to mention the horses and other wildlife." She had a dreamy expression on her face, which warmed Kody to his toes.

"Do *you* love it here," he asked, hoping for a positive answer.

She pulled her sweater around herself and faced him. "I think," she paused, and he held his breath. "I think that's a yes," she said, obviously teasing him. "It is so wonderfully beautiful, and incredibly peaceful. I would live out here – in a heartbeat," she said, watching him closely.

He grinned. He knew he did, but he couldn't help himself. Dare he imagine that one day Molly and Madison might live here on the ranch with him? His heart soared. That would be beyond all expectations.

And to think, none of this would have happened if he hadn't hit his head.

Chapter Six

They drove back into town in relative silence.

As they got closer, Kody had a sudden thought. "What if," he said, glancing across at her, "Instead of the two of us going out somewhere for dinner, we take the dinner to your place?"

Out the corner of his eye he saw her shift in her seat and clap her hands together. "What a wonderful idea!" She had a major grin on her face when he stole another glance. "Madison would *adore* that," she said. "For obvious reasons, she rarely leaves the apartment."

It made him sad that a young child didn't get to experience the world because of one inconsiderate person's actions.

His voice was quiet when he spoke. "I hope we can change that one day soon." He reached across and put his hand over hers. "Do you and Madison like fried chicken?"

"It's only her favourite," Molly squealed. Her excitement was palpable, and it was all he could do to stop himself pulling to the side of the road and pull her into a big bear hug.

They pulled into the carpark, and Kody parked the truck. Molly sat where she was seated. "Aren't you coming in?" he asked curiously.

"Sorry, I was lost in my thoughts," she said. "Like how long it will take for Chase to track Madison's father down, and ensure she is safe." She rubbed at her eyes, and he realised how much it had affected her emotionally.

Kody went around to her side of the truck and opened the door, pulling her into the bear hug he'd been wanting to give her for the past twenty minutes. This was mostly about comforting Molly when she most needed it, but it helped him as well.

"Okay," he said after a few minutes. "Bucket loads of fried chicken with all the trimmings." He grinned broadly. It was nice to have someone to spoil. That it turned out to be two someone's was even better.

In a relatively short time, he'd gone from being an almost total recluse, to craving for Molly's company when he wasn't with her.

He didn't in a million years dream that would ever be the case.

Standing at the counter he ordered the biggest bucket of fried chicken they had, mash and gravy, buns, fries, and bottles of soda. Molly protested loudly about how much it was going to cost, but Kody was having none of it.

89

"Isn't a man allowed to spoil his girls occasionally?" he asked. Molly's head went up and she stared into his eyes.

"Am I your girl?" she asked quietly, and he pulled her close to him.

He leaned down and gently kissed her on the lips. "Are you," he asked. "Because I sure hope you are." He gazed into her eyes, then kissed her forehead.

"Hey, hang on," Molly suddenly said. "You said girls. With an 's'." She looked at him suspiciously.

Kody laughed. Then kissed her again. "I included Madison," he said softly. "I hope one day we'll all be one big happy family."

Tears sprang to Molly's eyes, and she turned her head into Kody's chest. He knew she wouldn't want to make a scene, so they moved away from the counter while they waited for their food.

"Molly," he said quietly. "Madison is your niece. The two of you are a package deal. I get that, and I wouldn't have it any other way." He watched as the tears rolled down her cheeks.

She put her arms up around his back and put her head to his shoulder. "Kody," she said, barely audible, "You are a very special man."

Kody suggested they make it an indoor picnic, so Molly spread a tablecloth on the apartment floor.

Karen produced some plates and cutlery, along with napkins, and they all settled in.

"I can't wait for the day when we can have a real picnic," he whispered in Molly's ear. "Madison will be thrilled."

She smiled at him, and his heart soared.

It didn't take a lot for him to be happy these days – a simple smile from Molly, and he was over the moon.

Madison sat herself between Molly and Kody, snuggling as close to Molly as she could get. "Where do you live, Mr Kody?" she asked innocently.

He grinned at Molly. "On a farm," he said. "With lots of mountains, and paddocks, and horses."

The child screamed. "I love horses," she squealed, jumping up to stand next to him, then suddenly looked at him suspiciously. "Real horses or toy horses," she asked, not so sure anymore.

"Real horses," he said, and she grinned.

"Can I pat them?" she asked.

Kody sought Molly's permission, and she nodded. "One day you can come to my farm, and you can pat my horse. You can even feed him some carrot if you like."

He was surprised when Madison began to run around the room. "Can I Molly, can I?" she chanted as she continued to run.

Kody leaned over and whispered in Molly's ear and she nodded. Madison suddenly stopped and watched him closely.

"It's rude to whisper," she suddenly said, glaring at him.

Kody chuckled. "Yes, it is," he told the toddler. "I wanted to ask Molly if it was okay to say you could ride my horse Cracker when you visit."

She stood there staring at Kody, then Molly, then back to Kody.

"What did she say," the child asked quietly.

He grinned. "She said yes." His heart beat wildly wondering how Madison would react.

"Reeeeeeeeeeeeeeeaaaaaaaaaaaaaaaaaaaaalllll llllllly?" Madison jumped up and down on the spot and ran to Kody and hugged him. Then hugged Molly.

Lastly, she ran to Karen. "Did you hear," she asked Karen excitedly. "I'm going to ride Cracker!"

"That's wonderful," Karen told her. "Maybe you should sit down and eat your dinner now."

Madison nodded then went back to her place, moving a little closer to Kody this time.

He was bemused by the antics of the little girl and looked forward to them being one big happy family.

"You're healing beautifully, and can go home in the morning, Mr Carson," Molly told her elderly patient. "Would you like me to call your daughter to make the arrangements?"

He looked up at her in appreciation. "That's so nice of you Dr Simpson. Thanks so much."

Molly scribbled a note to remind herself to call, then moved onto the next patient.

She pulled the dressing back and carefully inspected the stitched area. "I'm sorry, Mr Watson," she said. "This wound is infected. I'll start you on IV antibiotics." She frowned at him appropriately. "Nurse." She waved the nurse over and handed her the patient's chart. "I've written Mr Watson up for IV antibiotics. You'll need to clean and redress the wound as well. Thank you," she said.

Molly continued on her rounds for another half hour, then thoroughly exhausted, went back to her office to write up all her notes, and finish off some paperwork.

93

She'd just swallowed the last mouthful of her coffee when her cell phone rang. "Molly Simpson."

"Molly," the caller said. "It's Chase. Sheriff Chase Callahan," he added, as though she may have forgotten who he was.

Her heart beat wildly, and she felt sweat bead on her upper lip. "Yes?" she said breathlessly. Was this the news she was waiting for?

She felt lightheaded. Being a doctor, Molly knew she was experiencing anxiety, and took long calming breaths. It seemed to help.

"I can be there in five, if it suits you," he said. "I don't want to interrupt..." He didn't get to finish the sentence.

"That's fine," she said quickly. "I'm at the hospital," she said, in case he didn't know.

The call ended, and she went back to her paperwork. She tried, she really did, but her thoughts were elsewhere.

Instead of stressing while she waited, Molly made herself a fresh mug of coffee. Extra strong. She leaned back and took a sip of the brew.

Despite expecting it, she startled when a knock came at the door. "Molly," he called gently.

"Come in, Sheriff," she answered. She stood and shook his hand. "Please, sit down." Until that moment she hadn't noticed Deputy Chris Dolan was there with him. "Deputy," she said, acknowledging the other man.

"I take it the news isn't good?" She sat looking into her hands, which were clasped together on the desk.

"I guess that depends on how you look at it," the deputy responded.

Chase spoke next. "We had to get the state police involved, since it's not our state, and not our jurisdiction.

Molly's heart sank. Were they going to tell her there was nothing they could do? Instead of putting her fears into words, she nodded.

"Madison's father," Chase began. "You were right, he's a drug addict."

Molly let go the breath she didn't know she was holding. So they'd caught up with him. She felt tears prickle at the back of her eyes, but she wouldn't let them flow.

She couldn't lose Madison to that monster no matter what. She had legal custody, so it shouldn't happen, but the bastard has been trying to get her back since the judgement.

"Molly," Chase said quietly. "Did you hear what I said?"

She put her fingers to her eyes and brushed at the errant tears. Damn her emotional state!

"No, I'm sorry, I was lost in my thoughts." She frowned at him. "I'm really sorry. This has been a difficult time."

Chase nodded. "I understand, I really do. And I do have news to give you." He settled back in his chair. "It's been confirmed by several sources," he told her. "Madison's father is...."

Molly put her hands to her eyes. Did she really want to hear this?

She felt a hand to her back and realized Chase had come around behind the desk and had squatted down to her level.

"Molly," he said softly beside her ear. "It's good news." His hand stayed on her back, and she felt somewhat comforted. "He's dead. Died from a drug overdose six months ago."

Molly sobbed into her hands.

Epilogue

Madison stood on a crate feeding carrots to Cracker.

Kody stood beside her with his hand to her back, ensuring she didn't fall.

Her little hand reached out to pat Cracker's face but faltered as she got closer. "It's alright, Madison," he told her gently. "He won't bite, I promise." She looked up at him with innocent eyes, and he marvelled at how lucky he was to have found his instant family.

"Do I get to ride him today?" Madison asked, eager to have her first ever horse ride.

Kody looked to Molly, and their eyes connected. "First we have to go into town and buy your riding gear," Kody told her. "I don't want you to get hurt if you fall off."

Madison scowled. "I won't fall off," she said, still scowling at him.

"Maddie, honey," Molly said. "You don't get to ride until you have the right gear. Understood?"

She stomped her foot on the crate and burst into tears in a three-year-old's tantrum. Kody grabbed her before she fell to the ground.

She looked at him with tears rolling down her face and wrapped her little arms around his neck. "I want to ride the horsey," she told him, mouth pouting.

His eyes were laughing, but he kept a straight face as he replied. "Of course you do, Madison. And you will. Just not right now." He gently nudged at her back and she relaxed into him.

"Time for lunch, and then we go and buy your riding clothes," Molly told her, stroking the little girl's long hair.

"She's nearly asleep," Kody whispered to Molly.

Madison quickly sat up. "No I'm not!"

Kody revelled in his new life, with his new little family.

Molly busied herself organising for the family party Kody had decided to hold.

No longer the family recluse, he'd invited all his brothers and their partners.

They'd bought a sparkling party dress for Madison, and Kody was in his best clothes. Molly had chosen an off-the-shoulder A-line style of dress, in the softest of pinks.

He'd told the family to wear 'neat casual' when the invitations went out, which he was sure would have them all scratching their heads.

Madison was overly excited at the thought of a party and couldn't keep still. She also utilized the full-length mirror on several occasions, to check out her pretty party dress.

Three trucks pulled up in the newly fenced parking area almost at the same time. "They're here, they're here," Madison shouted as she ran around the ranch house. She grabbed for Kody's hand. "Do I get to see baby Chloe today," she asked, her little eyes sparkling with wonder.

He squatted down to her level. "Yes, you do," he said. "You sure do."

She reached out and gave him a hug, with the biggest smile on her face.

Rory and Missy arrived first, baby Chloe sound asleep. They were both so very proud of their little offspring. Then came Jordon and Grace, and last to arrive was Chase and Isabella.

Deputy Chris Dolan had also been invited, since he was a close family friend. Unfortunately, he'd been called out on a case and wouldn't arrive until later.

Once everyone was seated in the outside area, Kody glanced across to Aunt Lizzie who was doing the catering for the party.

99

She had a big grin on her face and nodded to him. She lifted a glass and tapped it with a spoon, trying to get everyone's attention.

They all stopped talking, and everyone looked to Aunt Lizzie. "Kody has an announcement," she said, still grinning broadly.

"Ah, Molly and I have something to tell you," he said, looking across at her. "We, ah,"

"I know, I know," Madison squealed. "We got married today!"

Kody pulled Molly to him, the two laughing at Madison's impromptu announcement. He pulled her into a big bear hug and kissed her deeply, until Madison forced her way in. "Eeeeew!" she said, then put her little arms up for Kody to pick her up so she could join in the hug.

The End

Enjoy this story?

Check out the Callahan Brothers great-great grandmother Bessie's story:

Bessie – The Soiled Doves Series

https://www.amazon.com/Bessie-Soiled-Doves-Book-8-ebook/dp/B077BZQZXT/

For a full list of the Callahan Brothers Series

https://www.amazon.com/gp/product/B078W9YCP5?ref=series_rw_dp_labf

Check out <u>Cheryl's Amazon page</u> –

https://www.amazon.com/author/cherylwright

for a full list of her other books.

Other Links:

http://cheryl-wright.com

https://www.facebook.com/cherylwrightauthor

<u>Join my newsletter</u>

http://cheryl-wright.com/newsletter.html

About the Author

Multi-published, award-winning author, Cheryl Wright, former secretary, debt collector, account manager, writing coach, and shopping tour hostess, loves reading.

She writes both contemporary and historical western romance, as well as romantic suspense.

She lives in Melbourne, Australia, and is married with two adult children and has six grandchildren.

When she's not writing, she can be found in her craft room making greeting cards.